CLARENCL ....
SCREAMING MOUSE

Everyone knows mice can't fly, right?

By Major Treble

Dedication

I want to dedicate the book to my mother, Lola Mae Vincent

And acknowledge Julie Zeitlin the real miss Julie whose

house and backyard are where our story took place and

her beautiful cat Saki lived.

"A mother is your first friend, your best friend,

and your forever friend."

Acknowledgment

I want to thank everyone who came together to make this

book possible. It has been a pleasure working with my

editor and publisher, who worked hard with me to put this

project together. It's been a long road.

About the Author

I am a California born and raised boy. I played football and

baseball at highland high school in Bakersfield, California,

but I really wanted to play music. My mother and father

gave my brother, Mike, and me a sears guitar for Christmas

when I was 13, and that started it all. If you saw me back

then, when I had a guitar, I taught myself to play and sing,

trying to sound like the Beatles or Merle haggard. I played

in a couple of high school bands. Later on, I started playing

more serious bands such as full moon, and then forty-five.

We moved to Los Angeles in1979 to make it big we did well

but didn't get the brass ring eventually, we broke up, and I

went to play guitar for a band called the heartbeats. I then

met and married my first wife, Vicki, and decided I was a

country artist. I recorded a record titled a wanted man for

curb records. I toured the country, opening for some fine

acts and headlining some clubs. I made two videos that

were played on CMT. I played the super dome in New

Orleans, but the biggest show I did was the July 4 show in

Jacksonville, Florida, with Patti loveless and 38 specials for

a crowd of 20 thousand. I continued to play at smaller

shows and writing songs until everything just kind of

stopped. I met my second wife, Paula, and we moved to

Memphis. I made a lot of friends in Memphis and got to

know and play with some fine musicians; after about ten

years, we were divorced, and I moved back to Nashville, and

then the hammer fell on my head on June 8, 2013. I had a

hemorrhagic stroke and suffered left side paralysis. I

survived, but everything was different; I was depressed for

a time but figured, "Hey, I can still write!" so I started

coming up with ideas, Clarence being the first.

Prologue

Everyone has some hidden powers inside them. Only if you

could truly recognize them, imagine, what could you have

not achieved?

Let's turn the pages to discover the hidden powers of

Clarence. Let his life inspire you, and let yours inspire

others.

Everyone knows mice can't fly, right?

Clarence did not appear to be unusual in any way. In fact, he seemed ordinary in every way. He had whiskers that twitched to sample the world around him. Ears just large enough to alert him to any dangers that might be nearby and fur that helped him hide if he needed to. Yes, he was average on the outside, but he had something extraordinary on the inside. He didn't know it yet, but he was about to find out how extraordinary.

any wonderful creatures live in this great big world, and Clarence hadn't seen them all But he had seen some very interesting ones nearby. He had seen dogs, other mice, rats, birds, bugs and even snakes. To Clarence though, the most intriguing creatures were people. Some people were afraid of him. He, being so small and not so dangerous, couldn't believe that people were afraid of him.

Miss Julie was a person who lived in a house near Clarence. He thought houses were wonderful. They were warm in the winter and had plenty of places to explore and FOOD! Sometimes though, people had cats. Miss Julie had a cat named Saki so Clarence was always extra alert around her house.

One spring day Clarence could see Miss Julie in her backyard watering her plants and rearranging her patio table and talking to someone. Clarence hid under a hydrangea near the house where he could get a better look. Miss Julie was talking to Saki. Knowing what he knows about cats Clarence kept his distance. But he couldn't help notice how pretty Saki was and how she seemed to like Miss Julie a lot. She would get close to Miss Julie and rub against her leg and just look up at her and blink and Miss Julie would talk soft and sweet to

Saki. It almost looked like they loved each other! That just

mystified Clarence. If Miss Julie was afraid of him, a mouse,

why wasn't she afraid of Saki, a cat?

Cats are dangerous, mice are not, Clarence thought.

He decided to go exploring. Maybe he could find some birds. Clarence could watch birds all day. He loved to watch them fly high up into the trees or low over the grass in search of their favorite meal; bugs. Clarence would often daydream that he could fly just like the birds he loved to watch." Magnificent creatures" he would say to himself. They can go anywhere they want. 'Oh it would be awesome if I could fly,' he thought. Clarence knew all too well that he couldn't though. Everyone knows mice can't fly.

Later that afternoon Clarence was still exploring when he noticed a mockingbird flying low and close to something near a bush behind Miss Julie's house. He moved closer to see what that bird was interested in and he saw it was Saki. Clarence had never seen a bird do what this mockingbird was doing. That bird was diving down very close to her. "What a brave bird," he thought. While Clarence was watching all of this in amazement, he was not paying attention to where he was. He had always been taught to beware of being out in the open. But in an instant Saki turned to run from the

mockingbird and was running right at Clarence. Saki saw

Clarence and snatched him up in a flash!

Clarence was terrified. He was in the mouth of a cat! He could feel her warm, moist breath that smelled like cat food. Clarence did not want to be cat food though, under any circumstances. Saki took him into Miss Julie's house through a little door just for cats. Saki didn't usually eat the things she brought into the house but Clarence didn't know that. Luckily for Clarence, once Saki got him into Miss Julie's house, she lost interest in him and decided to go to the window to see if that mockingbird was still outside. Saki just dropped Clarence on the floor near the piano in Miss Julie's house. HIDE, he thought to himself,

get under the piano! So, he hurried and crawled under the

piano just as fast as he could.

Clarence hid for one whole night inside Miss Julie's house under that piano. Saki knew he was there though. She could smell him and hear every little frightened breath he took. She crouched and stared at the space under the piano waiting for him to come out. Miss Julie knew what that meant. Whenever she saw Saki so interested in the piano, or anything else something could hide under, it meant there was something hiding under it.

Oh no, thought Miss Julie, Saki has something trapped under the piano.

Miss Julie knew she had to see what it was and try to catch it and take it back out to the yard. I hope it's not a mouse, she thought to herself, I'm scared of mice. Clarence was scared of her too though. People are really big up close, he thought. Clarence didn't know what to do. I don't want to die under this piano in a house, he thought!

Clarence had to do something. He wasn't going to just give up. He decided he would make a run for it. Just then he heard Miss Julie coming toward the piano. He peeked out and saw that she had a broom. She tried to scoot him out from under the piano very gently. He ran! Clarence ran for all he was worth and scurried up the curtains on the window next to the piano.

He ran so fast he was a blur. Up into the curtains he climbed, as high as a mouse could climb and he hid in a pleat. Just then Saki leapt onto the window sill trying to catch

Clarence. "No" Miss Julie said firmly to Saki, "You've caused

enough trouble for one day". Miss Julie put Saki in a

bedroom and closed the door. She was going to catch

Clarence or help him get back outside without Saki's help.

Remember earlier we talked about how Clarence was an ordinary mouse? Well, he is on the outside, but Clarence knew he had to do something extraordinary to get out of this mess. He was so scared that his heart beat like a thousand tiny drums, so he reached way down inside of himself, into that place we all have where extraordinary things live, and Clarence found the strength to do something awesome: something he didn't even know he could do.

M

iss Julie swallowed hard, because she was scared too, and reached to pull the curtain back to see where Clarence was. "Ahhhhhhhhh", he screamed as loud as he could from above Miss Julie with all his might. At the same time he leaped as high as a mouse ever has and just flew! To his, and Miss Julie's, amazement Clarence screamed and flew across the living room toward the door that Miss Julie had left open. Miss Julie screamed too. She thought Clarence was on the floor not up high in the curtain. In all of her life she had never heard a mouse scream or fly! Today though

Miss Julie saw, and heard, a flying screaming mouse.

Clarence was flying, if only for a moment, just like the birds he loved to watch. He landed on the floor and ran out the door as fast as he could back into the yard and into the bushes where he lived. He was so grateful to be home safe and sound Clarence kissed every creature he saw right on the lips.

The End

Made in the USA
Coppell, TX
23 February 2021

50724767R00020